Emma
&
The Sea Creatures

Book Cover Concept: Tiffany Nixon
Interior Concept: Tiffany Nixon
Illustrations: © Tiffany Nixon

Publisher: VMH Publishing

Paperback ISBN: 978-1-947928-40-4

Manufactured in the United States of America

10 9 8 7 6 5 4 3 2 1

Dedication

I dedicate this book to my remarkable children who inspired me to pursue a career in writing. I love all of you. If it wasn't for them waking me up in the morning saying, "Mom what about your book?" I would've not gotten to this point where I'm currently at now. I lost hope. I thought no one would think to read what I've created but I was completely wrong. My children believed in me when I didn't believe in myself.

I use to think what I wrote was either weird or boring but I was wrong again. As I finished writing this book and read it to my children, all they could do were clap and tell me how much they love me and my book. So now I'm like, "Wait a minute! You love my book more than me?" They shrugged their shoulders but nevertheless I was pleased to know they enjoyed reading my finished manuscript.

I also dedicate this book to my grandmother who passed away in 2012. She too inspired me to be who I am today. I never knew my grandmother believed in me so much until the day she was slipping away and could barely talk. But she managed to tell her nurse, "This my granddaughter. She's gonna be a writer and actor." This made me smile so much I left the hospital that day still smiling from my grandmother's peaceful words. I love you Granny and wish you were here to see my success.

Next I couldn't leave my mom out. She's the one who birthed me and tolerated all the kiddie things I did when I was a kid. Thanks Mom, for also believing in me when others didn't love you more mom.

And I love all my readers. Thanks for taking the time to pick up this book and read it. Love you all. Last but not least, thanks to all my family and friends who showed support towards me as I wrote this book. It wasn't easy at all, especially after giving birth to my children. But you all also believed and helped me push constantly. Love you all!

Chapter 1

Once upon a time there was an eight year old girl named Emma. Emma lived a very comfortable lifestyle with her successful parents, Mr. Sunny and Mrs. Sunny.

Mr. Sunny and Mrs. Sunny spoiled Emma terribly, 24/7, 365 days a year. Emma had many friends to play with during the day, yet she wasn't satisfied with them. Emma considered her friends as boring and useless.

Emma's friends couldn't do enchanting things like the sea creatures could do. Therefore, Emma ignored her friends on some occasions. Emma also often treated her parents poorly. Continuously' she showed them no respect. There were times when Emma was very unpleasant to be around.

Nevertheless, everyone that surrounded Emma cherished her no matter how ill- mannered she was towards them.

But Emma never worried about how her behavior made her family or friends feel. Emma only cared about living in the ocean with the sea creatures, since life didn't seem so complex for them.

Chapter 2

Emma went directly home after school. Of course she knew her parents weren't going to be there, due to their hectic work schedules.

"Hello my little angel I am so thrilled that you've arrived!" Mrs. Sunny voiced joyously.

Emma was shocked to see her mother at home so early, especially around two-thirty in the evening.

She must've forgotten something.

I am for certain she didn't come home early to be a loving, caring parent towards me, Emma said to herself.

"So Mom, what brings you home so soon?" Emma stated sarcastically, while folding her arms into a bow.

"Well, since you asked I'll tell you," her mother replied. "I thought it would be an awesome idea that I spent the rest of the day with you. We could do some mother and daughter things like, shopping for things your father wouldn't think twice to buy us," laughed Mrs. Sunny.

"Then we could make our way to the ocean for a swim," she added in delight.

"Yip-pee!!" Emma shouted like a five year old kid.

Emma wasn't passionate about the secretive shopping spree she was about to take with her mother. Every time they went shopping, her mom would wander off when she spotted a co-worker or friend she knew. She'd strike up a long conversation, forgetting all about Emma standing before her.

Therefore all the excitement Emma starred was only from her mother

mentioning they would take a dip in the ocean. Oh indeed Emma loves her mom dearly. But not as much as she loves the ocean. In Emma's mind the ocean is her first priority.

Chapter 3

Mrs. Sunny and Emma arrived at the shopping mall. It was very crowded with after school children who lacked in manners. A young girl who looked to be in her teens, was skate boarding in the mall. The girl was having so much fun breaking the mall rules that she didn't see Emma and her mom walking towards her.

"Ouch wimp! Watch where you're going" Emma yelled in a rude manner, as the girl nearly knocked her off her feet.

"Oops! I am so...sorry" the girl replied with sincerity around her voice.

Emma didn't reply back when the girl apologized to her. Instead, she rolled her eyes at the girl. In that instance, the girl quickly strayed far away from Emma's cruel stare. Umph! I bet she'll watch were she's going next time Emma said to herself in a devilish tone.

"Emma what has gotten into you?!" Mrs. Sunny asked curiously.

"Well, to be honest Mom I am tired of living in this lifeless city. The kids are rude and they're NO FUN," Emma replied truthfully.

"I know this is a different environment than Nashville. But it's our home from here on out. We've resided in this city for almost five years now. Emma I think it's time for you to move on and enjoy the greatness this city has to offer" Mrs. Sunny stated with earnest surrounding her voice.

"Yeah alright...omg!" Emma flat out changed the subject when she spotted a bathing suit store.

"Mom, can we go please?" Emma inquired with puppy dog eyes.

"Yes we can go my little angel," Mrs. Sunny uttered nicely.

Once they entered the store, Emma was dazzled by all the different bathing suits. Emma chose five swimming suites then narrowed it down to one. It was a light blue two- piece suit that had fishes printed on it.

Mrs. Sunny purchased the bathing suit. Then they both exited the store. "Tina, Tina over here," a squeaky voice cried out to Mrs. Sunny. She looked over to her left and knew exactly who was calling out to her. Only one person would call her by her first name and that somebody would be Jazzy.

The familiar woman began to walk towards Mrs. Sunny and Emma like she was trying to win a walk-a-thon. Omg! Not again, Emma said to herself when Jazzy approached them.

"Hhh-" Jazzy uttered incompletely before Mrs. Sunny cut her off.

"Unfortunately I don't have any time to stay and chat," Informed Mrs. Sunny "I'll call you later."

They agreed to give each other a call later then said their goodbyes. Everyone then exited the mall.

Mm... I can't believe Mom didn't abandon me this time to go talk to her big mouth friends. Maybe it's something in the water, Emma voiced to herself with a giggle.

Chapter 4

"Mom can you please... step on the gas," Emma begged her mother. "Emma I am going the speed limit. I refuse to get a speeding ticket because you're in a rush to dive in the ocean," her mother said sternly.

I refuse to get a speeding ticket, Emma mimicked her mother's words amongst herself, while sitting in the back seat kicking her mother's seat.

"Emma, now cut that out I am trying to drive. We're almost home," Mrs. Sunny voiced.

Mrs. Sunny stopped at a red traffic light. She then turned her head to demand Emma to stop kicking her seat. When Emma decided to stop being a rascal, her mother immediately pressed her foot on the gas pedal leaving tire marks on the concrete.

Mrs. Sunny was so frustrated with Emma's actions that she overlooked a mother duck crossing the street with her ducklings. "Mom don't hit the ducks!" Emma blurted out loudly.

Her mother briskly hit the brakes causing Emma to fall onto the floor of the backseat, while scaring the ducks away.

"Emma are you okay"? Mrs. Sunny inquired in a frightened voice .

"I am ok mom"! Emma replied rudely, removing herself from the floor.

Maybe if she would've kept her eyes glued on the road, this would've never happened, Emma thought to herself. Mrs. Sunny could sense something was bothering Emma, due to the facial expression and the silence she held. For that reason, Mrs. Sunny didn't want to disturb Emma's quiet time. So she drove home in silence.

!!!
CKIIIT!!!

Chapter 5

When Mrs. Sunny and Emma arrived home they unpacked their bags quickly, so they could go to the ocean. Emma put on her swimming suit, and so did her mother. Then they were on their way to the ocean. Without a pause, Emma dived into the ocean leaving her mother behind.

Emma swam with assorted fish and other swimmers. Emma had So much fun in the ocean that she stayed in the water for forty five minutes. She thought it would be a fine idea if she took a small break from the water, therefore she swam back to dry land.

Emma grabbed her huge beach towel and wrapped it around her child size body. After she was completely dry, Emma decided to dig her hand into the sand. While Emma made a sand castle, she hummed to herself, la, la, la...while creating a Barbie doll size sand box.

Suddenly the wind began to blow at a rapid speed, causing Emma to lose her twenty four karat gold bracelet her mother and father gave her. Emma didn't notice as the bracelet shifted off her tiny wrist because she was having too much fun building her sand castle.

Emma suddenly noticed her bracelet was missing from her wrist. She started digging in the sand for it. After fifteen minutes of shoving her tiny hands through the sand Emma finally gave up searching for her precious bangle.

Out of nowhere she spotted something shiny in the sand that resembled her bracelet. Emma then walked over to the shiny mysterious item. But to her surprise it wasn't her bracelet.

It was a wand!

Chapter 6

After Emma discovered the wand, she stood there pondering whether she should pick it up. What's the worse can happen, she said to herself. Emma collected the wand and begins to twirl it around in circles.

Out of the blue, sparks and smoke circulated around Emma. She begins to cough and wave smoke from around her. After all the sparks and smoke disappeared, Emma started to walk away slowly from the wand hoping she wouldn't get any more surprises.

As Emma started walking away she heard a tiny voice cry out for help."Someone please help me," the voice called out.

"Where are you?" Emma asked in a confused manner. Emma searched for the voice until she found the person who was

calling out for help. When Emma identified the tiny person, she was indeed terrified because she'd never seen a tiny person with wings before.

Emma assured herself that she wasn't going to help this tiny person. Emma then heard the person call out for help once more. That's when Emma reconsidered her decision. She bends down and scooped the tiny person from the sand, while tapping the person on the back.

After Emma saw that the little person was stable, she assisted with some fresh water. It was like magic! The aid Emma provided helped in a major way because the tiny person recovered rapidly.

"Thank you so much for your help," said the tiny person. Oh! By the way my name is Ultra. And I am a fairy princess," she uttered politely while extending her hand.

You're very welcomed," Emma replied while shaking Ultra's hand.

"Are you out here alone?" Ultra asked in a concerned manner.

"No! I am not alone. My mother is over there," Emma stated, pointing to her mother.

"Ohhh... I see," Ultra voiced.

"So where did you come from? Where are your mom and dad? How did you get here? And how old are you?" Emma asked puzzled.

"Slow...down!" Ultra reacted.

"One question at a time. First, I am From a small island called Fairy's Island. That's where my pixie mom and dad live. Second, I've been patiently searching for my brother who's been lost for over a year now," informed Ultra.

"I was told he could be found in Tennessee.

But somehow I got lost during a storm. That's how I ended up here.

And third, I am fifty two years old. I know what you're thinking. I look pretty swell for my age. But I didn't do it alone. I use fairy skin crème," Ultra said with a giggle.

Ultra wasn't like most of the fairy princesses form Fairy's Island. All the other fairy princesses on the island had snobby attitudes, blue hair, red lips, pink freckles, big feet, big hands, and large elf ears. Now Ultra on the other hand, was a sweet, gentle, loving fairy that captured the hearts of other fairies on the island.

Whenever a fairy was sad, Ultra would place a tender kiss on it's cheek.

Instantly, the fairy's saddened face would turn upside down. Whenever Ultra did a good deed, her cheeks would glow like a light bulb. That really upset the other fairies, being that Ultra had a brilliant shine about herself. The other fairies had dark clouds lunging over their heads due to their nasty demeanors.

Every time Ultra had a good day another fairy would try to ruin it, by saying Little Feet and other rude slurs towards her. But Ultra didn't listen to their rude comments. She was well aware that the other fairies were jealous of her, because they all treated her so mean. Unfortunately that wasn't the case. The other fairies admired Ultra's beauty. Ultra was different from them all. Her characteristic features consisted of orange hair, pink lips, orange freckles, little feet, little hands, small elf ears, and a beautiful attitude like a rainbow. For that reason Ultra was talked about constantly by other fairies. But she didn't let their un- pleasant behavior control who she was. Ultra continued to be a kind loving fairy, very dissimilar from the rest.

Chapter 7

"I can't believe how far you've traveled just to find your long lost brother," Emma voiced surprisingly.

"Oh yes! My dear as the oldest fairy daughter it's my mission to care for my younger siblings. If they go wondering off it's my job to search for them," Ultra stated with confidence.

"So where do you go from here, now that you haven't found your bother around here?" Emma said oddly.

"I guess I'll search somewhere else until I find him," Ultra responded.

If you don't mind, I would definitely like to help you find your brother," Emma offered sincerely.

"Oh No! I don't mind. "I could use all your help," Ultra replied happily. Emma and Ultra searched high and low for Ultra's brother. Sadly they 42 came up with nothing. Therefore they were ready to call it a day, because they were very exhausted and hungry.

All of a sudden fireworks began to shoot in the sky just a few miles from where Emma and Ultra stood. The commotion brought them out of zombie mode and into reality.

"Hey do you see those exquisite explosives?" Emma asked Ultra in a childlike way.

"Yes! I did they're fantastic," Ultra replied.

"Come on what are you waiting for, permission from our parents?" Emma asked sarcastically as she began to move towards the fireworks. OH! She's fast, but faster than me, Ultra said to herself as she flew straight pass Emma.

"Hey that's not fair," Emma yelled loudly.

"Yeah your right. It's not fair, so hop on my back," Ultra voiced.

Emma hopped on Ultra's back with fear written all over her face. She was absolutely frightened being that she was much bigger than Ultra. Emma thought she would break Ultra's mini back. But since Ultra insisted, Emma got on her back as she was told.

All of a sudden Ultra began to stretch and grow. She became twice the size of Emma's mom even. Then up in the air Ultra fly with Emma holding on tight, bursting in exhilaration.

"Omg! It's amazing, " Emma uttered jumping up and down like she won a prize as the approached the fireworks.

"I agree Emma. It's wonderful," Ultra responded as her eyes lit up like Christmas lights.

"So what's the plan?" Emma questioned.

"Well since this place is overcrowded I think we'll have to split up," Ultra uttered. "Um...okay!" Emma agreed.

Emma headed towards the big crowd of people while Ultra stood at the front entrance and exit passage way. She knew it wasn't possible for anyone to escape the festival, unless they passed by her since the place was surrounded with gates and fences. For this reason she would have a greater opportunity in finding her lost brother.

Emma made her way through the crowd by pushing and shoving people just to get a better glance of the action. Once she made it to the stage, her rude behavior stopped when she saw dwarfs juggling fishes. At the same time they were using blow torches to fry the fish and serve it to the hungry crowd of people.

Emma was aroused by the thrill of it all. She'd never seen dwarfs juggling

sea- food before. After seeing their talents, she wanted to join them on stage.

"Let me try," Emma repeated over and over again until she was recognized by the jugglers. They called her to the stage. She was more than willing to go on and participate. Emma didn't accept any assistance from the jugglers. In her mind, he was a better juggler than the dwarfs any- way. Without a doubt she would prove it to them.

Instead of juggling three fish like the dwarfs, Emma decided to juggle six fish. There were OH's and Aah's from the crowd.

This only increased her confidence to a higher level.

Chapter 8

Mmm... I wonder who she is, the boy said to himself. After Emma's performance was over, the boy approached Emma.

"Um... excuse me. That was a remarkable performance you gave," the boy said.

"Why thanks!" Emma replied.

"So what's your name?" asked the boy impatiently.

"My name is Emma," she said.

"And my name is Violet," he replied as he flapped his wings.

"If I am wrong correct me; but do you have a sister name Ultra?" Emma asked anxiously, with a smile glued to her face.

"Yes! That's my sister, but how do you know she's my sister?" Violet questioned.

"Ultra told me about you when me and her first met. But it's a confusing story how we met, so I'll give you the details later. At the present time, the most important thing is getting you back home because Ultra really loves and misses you a lot," Emma stated seriously.

"Yeah I know she does. But when I am at home I can never leave her sight. Since I am the youngest fairy in the family and she's the oldest fairy, so she's like my protector. It's like being hooked to a breathing machine and struggling to breathe when I am around her," Violet said sadly.

"Now there's no need to be sad, because Ultra is only trying to protect you from bad people," Emma reassured.

CIRCUS

"Yeah I guess you're right. I do need to go back home," Violet said grinning.

"Well come with me, your sister is right this way," Emma voiced. Just before they could move a muscle Ultra found them.

"Hey there you are Emma. I've been looking all over fo-" Ultra started. She couldn't finish her sentence being that she got tongue tied from seeing Violet pop out from behind Emma.

"Where have you been little brother? I've been searching all over for you since the day you disappeared," Ultra asked loaded with emotions."

"Um,.. " Violet muted with eyes full of tears. Give me a hug it doesn't matter where you've been, you're here now," Ultra said while giving him a kiss on the cheek.

Due to Emma's kindness by saving Ultra's life and finding her brother. Ultra was eager to grant Emma one wish. Before she granted Emma her wish, she advised Emma to wish wisely. Once her wish was granted, Emma couldn't take it back.

Emma made a wish without feeling guilty about manipulating Ultra. Deep down inside Emma felt no remorse towards Ultra's feelings or anyone else's. All she cared about was making her wish. After Emma made her wish she was now on her own, Ultra and Violet went back to Fairy's Island to rejoice Violet's return.

Chapter 9

Blup, blup, blup were the sounds that Emma made while trying to catch her breathe in the water. Emma was panicking. She'd noticed her body frame had changed from human to an aquatic animal. This is where Emma put on her thinking cap. Okay! What did I wish for? Let me think...... OH NO! this can't be happening, she said to herself.

Emma realized her wish was fulfilled. But it wasn't exactly what she'd wished for. Emma wished to join the sea creatures in the big blue ocean. But didn't want to become a sea creature. As she examined her body from neck down she became nauseated from looking at her appearance. Okay! Just breathe Emma, it could be worse than this, she uttered to herself.

Emma relaxed by taking some deep breaths. Moments later she adapted to her new look. Well it's not that bad. At least I can be overbearing towards the smaller fish, Emma thought to herself with a cruel giggle.

As Emma moved through the water searching for other fish to mingle with, she begins to sing a song she'd written when she was a human girl.

I am a little girl, trapped in a cruel World want to live in the sea, so I Can find pearls, play with the fish, OH! How I Wish I could be a fish, Fishy, fishy, fish.

Emma sung her song with her eyes closed. When she opened her eyes she was blissful with the crowd she had attracted.

"Wow! That was awesome," the catfish uttered happily.

"Well, I am glad you enjoyed it," Emma replied bashfully.

The fish moved closer towards Emma. This frightened her.Emma thought she was going to be attacked, therefore she started to back away slowly.

"Hey! Where are you going? We only want to be your friend," the blow fish stated, disappointed. Emma carefully thought about what the blow fish had just said to her.

"Well alright! My name is Emma," she said proudly.

"And my name is Whistle," the blow fish uttered while demonstrating the reason why its name is whistle.

After the Whistle got acquainted with Emma, the other fish introduced themselves to her as well.

"I am Five," the starfish said. I am Sugar," the jellyfish stated.

"I am Bony," the teleost fish said.

"And I am Length," the angler fish said.

There were so many different fish introducing themselves to Emma to the point where she couldn't possibly remember all their names. Emma was astonished at how many dissimilar fish there were in the ocean. There were starfish, angler fish, teleost fish, jelly fish and other different kinds of sea creatures that swiftly traveled through the ocean. And every fish had a nickname. This was unbelievable to Emma.

"Can anyone tell me the rules of the ocean?" Emma asked.

"Rules?" five the starfish replied while laughing hysterically.

Emma was extremely embarrassed for asking such a foolish question.

"It's isn't funny," Emma voiced.

"OH! It's quite funny, because there aren't any rules in the ocean. But

the only rule I would suggest to you newbie is to stay alive in these waters," Five the starfish warned.

"Of course I'll survive in this ocean. I don't have this sword attached to my face for no particular reason," Emma stated arrogantly with a smirk pasted to her face.

"Everything isn't as smooth as it seems in these waters. There are much bigger sea creatures than yourself in this ocean. And of course the bigger sea creatures always win. So you can stop acting all macho," Five the starfish said harshly.

"Well I live by my mommy's saying, little fish eat big fish because big fish bones have vanish," Emma stated with confidence.

Chapter 10

Five the starfish was trying to help Emma out by warning her about the bigger creatures in the water. But Emma was too stubborn to listen to anyone else's advice or rules but her own. Emma would soon reap the consequences of her selfishness.

Cruising the water in search of food, Emma was stopped and captured by a bunch of hungry white sharks.

"Well, well guys- look what we have here, a lost fishy," the shark voiced, showing its sharp pointy teeth. Emma was scared it was written all over her body gestures, being that Emma body trembled at a nonstop able speed.

"Um- Hi my name is Emma," she stated nervously hoping these sharks were friendlier than the sharks she'd seen on television.

"He, he, he... save the pathetic introduction because once we eat you, you won't even exist anymore," the hungry shark stated with an evil smirk.

I guess five was right all along I am not the strongest sea creature in the ocean, especially when it comes to these white sharks their bigger and a lot meaner than I am, Emma thought to herself.

"Okay! I have an idea," Emma suggested to the sharks.

"Were all ears," the sharks replied while invading Emma's personal space. OH! I hope this works if it doesn't I am about to be seafood, Emma said silently.

"Well when I use to be a human girl I use to play a game called paper-rock-scissors with my friends. The winner gets treated like a queen or king, and the losers become servants to the winner," Emma uttered trying to sound confident.

Wait just one minute!" replied the enraged shark. "You use to be a human?" he asked gritting its teeth.

"Um... yes," Emma replied on edge.

"Now that gives us every reason to eat you. We don't like humans since all they do is trap us sharks to do experiments that are supposed to cure illnesses in human children. But their little experiments don't seem to be working because I've lost count of how many sharks are disappearing from the ocean. If their projects were really working then us sharks would be left alone so we could do our duties in the ocean as an eating machine," the agitated shark voiced.

"No, no- you're wrong! I am nothing like those humans. I cherish every sea creature. That's why I wanted to live in the ocean with you all. Because sea creatures are more warm hearted than humans are," Emma uttered sincerely.

Somehow Emma convinced the sharks that she was totally different compared to humans, therefore she got the sharks to play paper- rock- scissors.

"Paper- rock-scissors," Emma said. By this time there were only two sharks left in the game.

"Paper rock scissors! Nope you're out," Emma uttered. Now there was Emma and one shark left in the game.

"Paper rock scissors, oh! You're out, I won," Emma said flipping all around. This made the sharks angry, for losing to a swordfish.

"So this means I am a queen and you guys are slaves," Emma said boastfully.

The sharks looked at each other with only one thing on their minds, call the bet off and just eat Emma. But they wanted to be fair so they shook their heads in agreement.

"I guess you're right" the sharks stated.

"Now here's what I need you all to do for me-," Emma said. "Find me some food, get a mirror and show me around this ocean," Emma demanded.

Emma was new to the ocean so for that reason she took advantage of using the sharks while she could, before they eventually turned on her like pit bulls.

I don't know if I am going to like living in the ocean, Emma said to herself with a displeased look on her face.

After the sharks completed all assignments Emma demanded from them, the sharks then decided to let Emma go free. But not before they played a game of cat and mouse with her. The sharks chased Emma all around the ocean until they got tired.

Chapter 11

"Bop, bop, bop," eight the octopus sang in a jazz rhythm, while playing the saxophone, drums, and piano.

"Blow that horn Eight," the female dolphin shouted while tossing a ball on stage at Eight The Octopus as a gift to him.

Eight was having a live concert. As a result he captured a large audience from every sea creature there in the ocean and this included Emma as well. As she made her way towards the crowd, her head begin to move to the Rhythm.

Oh yeah! Now that's some great soul music, Emma said loudly to herself. It was like someone had Emma under a spell because she danced nonstop like a backup dancer. Emma didn't realize eight had stopped his performance.

At this point all the attention was focused on Emma. She danced and be-bopped to her own imaginary music that played in her head. When she finally realized eight had ceased his live performance, she felt embarrassed for stealing his moment. All the sea creatures glared at Emma with rage written all over their faces, due to her interrupting Eight's concert. This was the first concert he'd performed in the ocean. Since being on tour all the other concerts were held on dry land.

"Now, now there's no reason to get all violent," Emma uttered in fear.

"I don't know about everyone else here, but I have every reason to be upset at you. That's my pop-pa," the toddler octopus said, cascading tears. The gloomy speech the toddler octopus gave had the audience on edge like a volcano ready to blow.

All eyes begin to stare at Emma, this horrified her to the point she

started biting on her inner jaw and wagging her tail. Emma had to think of a clever plan before the other sea creatures smashed her like whipped potatoes. Oooh... why do I keep screwing up like this Emma thought to herself. Emma started exploring the ocean, looking for things she could use to make her plan work.

The angry crowd became jumbled from watching Emma search the ocean like a crazy treasure hunter. Once Emma collected everything she needed, she then took a short break to catch her breath.

The items Emma collected were jump ropes, frisbees, rotten apples, several bean bags, numerous limestone marbles, cones, horse shoes, blind folds and much more. Emma's clever ideas were beginning to intertwine together. She came up with an idea of having a field day for all the sea creatures to participate in. Emma thought this activity would be more interesting than a live concert.

Indeed Emma was right about the event she planned being that all the sea creatures were having a great time competing against each other. The first game started with tossing frisbees.

"Okay! Here's how you play, whoever tosses the frisbees the farthest wins," Emma stated excitedly.

"So what does the winner get?" the young sea horse asked spontaneously.

"Well the winner gets a bag full of earth worms I found," Emma replied.

"Yip-pee," the young sea horse uttered while doing backwards flips.

After the frisbee game was over it was time for the next game to begin. The blind folding game. Again Emma had to explain the rules of the game. Everyone was having such a fantastic time they didn't hear Emma scream for their attention.

"I said listen up for the second time," Emma said in a humorless manner. All the sea creatures focused their attention on Emma. But they all stared at Emma with mean expressions on their faces.

"Now that I have your attention these are the rules of the game. I need for everyone to listen closely because this game is a tad bit complexed," Emma voiced. All the sea creatures remained silent and listened closely as Emma explained the rules.

"Here I have several blind folds and marbles. The object of the game is to be blind folded while trying to find the floating marbles. Oh! And the winner gets a bag full of squishy lightning bugs," Emma explained. Once more the Sea Creatures jumped for joy after hearing what the winner receives for winning each game.

As the day grew older the sea creatures became exhausted from all the activities Emma provide for them, therefore they decided to call it quits for the day. But before Emma left she apologized for interrupting eight the octopus' concert. The Sea Creatures accepted her apology. Then everyone departed in separate directions.

Chapter 12

"Hey Sunny and Bright! Have you all seen Emma?" Sky asked the twin girls with concern surrounding her voice.

They both shook their heads no. Hump! I wonder where she's been hiding, Sky said to herself. The three friends decided to meet at the beach after school for a short swim, while the sun still beamed through the buffy clouds.

"Am I the only one who feels a little weird about this situation?" Sunny questioned.

"Um... I feel weird," Bright replied.

"So do me," Sky agreed.

Despite the fact Emma was very mean towards her friends, they still missed her presence.. After moping around for several minutes, the three friends decided to go for a swim. Once they were in the water their hopeless attitudes begin to fade away.

"Hey Sunny, pass me the ball?" Sky asked actively.

The girls started to have a blast playing a game of volleyball amongst themselves and other children their age. La, la, la, .. Emma hummed amongst herself while cruising through the ocean, surfacing in and out the water.

Emma noticed three girls having a great time passing a ball back and forth to each other. Ooh. .. that looks like a lot of fun, Emma uttered to herself. Emma swam a little closer towards the girls so she could get a better view.

Omg! It's my friends, Emma said to herself. She couldn't believe they were having fun without her.

"Wee......." the girls yelled loudly as they splashed water in each other's face.

After Emma saw her friends having so much fun without her, she instantly broke down and cried like a toddler.

All I wanted was to live in the ocean with the sea creatures; not become a sea creature and distance myself from my friends. Oh! What have I done to myself, I should've wished carefully, Emma spoke amongst herself. As she swamped away from the girls she use to know as her friends.

"Nooo..." Emma cried intensely as she was captured into a net.

"Uh huh guys we have a big one," the gigantic man said while showing his dingy teeth. Emma was seized by some stranded sailors who'd been lost in the sea for several months. These avid sailors survived by catching various sea animals.

Once the sailors hauled Emma on board, they released the net. Emma immediately fell on the floor of the boat.

Emma tried escaping, but it was no use since she was outnumbered by vicious sailor men and sailor women.

Ultra, if you can hear me I really can use your help, Emma uttered silently to herself with her eyes closed. Oh Shucks! I knew I should've listened to Ultra when she told me to wish carefully. Now I am stuck on this boat with some seafood lovers and Ultra isn't going to rescue me, Emma voiced sadly to herself. When she opened her eyes there was no sight of Ultra.

"Please let me go," Emma sang out softly.

"You hear that everyone? The little fishy wants us to let her go," the sailor said harshly with an evil laugh.

Suddenly Emma felt a sharp pain in her neck. She placed her hand on her neck to see if she'd been stung by a bee. But to her surprise the aching pain wasn't from a bee. It was from the tranquilizer the wicked sailor had injected in her. Within seconds Emma was sound asleep.

Chapter 13

After being asleep for quite some hours Emma finally woke up confused.

"Where am I," Emma asked the squid.

"We're in the middle of the Atlantic Ocean," the squid replied.

"Atlantic Ocean!" Emma shouted. Emma was emotionally disturbed from being so far away from home, to the point she was beginning to feel home sick.

"Oh! I feel sick," Emma stated to the squid, as food contents erupted from her stomach.

"Are you okay?" the squid asked in a concerned tone.

Emma shook her head yes.

"What's with all the racket?" the sailor asked glancing at Emma in a sickening manner.

"Um... I don't feel well," Emma replied.

"I am not concerned about how you feel. But if you don't behave yourself I will cook you for lunch. oh! And clean Up this mess," the sailor spoke unpleasantly.

After the sailor disappeared Emma got a rag from a bucket and begin cleaning up her mess.

"Do you need help?" the squid asked politely.

"Noo... Emma shouted roughly to the squid.

"Hey, I was only trying to help you out. There's no need to yell at me," the squid expressed glumly.

"You're right, I apologize for being mean," Emma said genuinely, then gave

the squid a hug.

Five days had passed and Emma was still aboard the boat with the cruel sailors. When darkness filled the sky Emma looked to the sky and made a wish upon a star. Emma wished she could go back home to her friends and family.

She no longer wanted to live in the ocean with the sea creatures, because it wasn't what she thought it would be.

Suddenly Emma was disturbed by a woman sailor. The woman approached Emma in a friendly manner. But Emma wasn't so jolly towards the woman.

"Stay away from me," Emma uttered to the woman, while backing away from her into a corner.

"Please calm down. I am only here to help you," the woman stressed.

"Okay explain yourself," Emma said.

"Alright. I am Amerika. My husband is in charge of everyone on this boat including myself. We've been stranded for a very long time. Everyone has been surviving off of fish and other sea creatures that live in the ocean. But lately we haven't had any luck catching anything. Therefore, our only solution in satisfying our hunger is to cook you! But I won't let that happen that's why I am here to rescue you," the woman said sincerely.

"How do I know this isn't a trick to get me in the fryer?" Emma asked.

"Oh this isn't a trick. I give you my word," the woman replied.

"Okay I believe you," Emma stated.

"Now give me your hand, and just follow me," the woman demanded. Emma did as told. As soon as they joined hands,the big bad sailors came barging in with butter knives, hot sauce, torches and napkins in their possessions.

"Noo........!" Emma cried out.

Chapter 14

"Emma, Emma wake up!" Sky called. "You're having a bad dream." Emma woke up rubbing her eyes to only see her friends and her mom surrounded around her.

"Wha... happened to me," Emma questioned them all.

"Oh! Honey you had a nasty accident when you and I went to the ocean for a swim," her mother said. Emma gazed around the room visioning a ton of flowers that were sent from people who adored her.

"Are all these flowers for me?" Emma asked her mother.

"Yes my little angel all these flowers are for you," her mother replied with a huge grin on her face.

Emma grabbed a card from a yellow Lilly. After reading the card she felt selfish for treating those around her like they were nothing to her. Hastily Emma started to day dream about the dream she'd had.

"Emma snap out of it," her mother voiced.

"Mom I had an unrealistic dream that was very weird. Sky, Sunny and Bright were in my dream," Emma vented.

"Emma, it was only a dream. There's nothing to worry about," her mother assured.

At that moment Emma begin to wonder what it would be like if her dream became true. There's no other place I rather be than in Florida Emma said to herself.

"Everyone gather around there's something I need to say. Um... I know I haven't been a great friend or an

Well
Soon!
Get
Well

appreciative daughter. But I want you all to know I love you all," Emma stated sincerely.

"Aww...everyone uttered then gave Emma a hug. Emma realized being in the ocean with the sea creatures wasn't more important than her family and friends. She promised herself and everyone else that she'll never be self-centered and rude again.

Chapter 15

Nine years later...

Emma was now a young adult. She'd just turned twenty years old. Emma managed to graduate high school, and attended college shortly after. Emma obtained a teacher's degree. She landed a great career teaching middle school children.

"Now settle down students. I have some guest that'll be joining our class today," Emma voiced.

The guest had finally arrived. Emma opened the door and came in Sky, Sunny and Bright. The three women introduced them- selves to the students.

"I need everyone's full attention today, because these ladies took time out of their busy schedules to be here today. Also, they will be assisting me with different activities I have planned today," Emma said to her students, then grabbed a book from out of her desk.

I need everyone to get a chair and move towards the front of the classroom. I'm about to read a book called Emma and The Sea Creatures," Emma said happily.

"What's this book about?" a student asked.

"Well... It's about a young girl who realized family and friends are more important than living in the ocean with the Sea creatures," Emma replied, winking at her friends.

Emma and her longtime friends took turns reading the book to the students. After the story was over, the students clapped their hands and asked plenty of questions about the story.

"Um, I wonder if the students will understand the lesson from this book. I hope so because they should know that family and friends are more valuable than anything, Emma said to herself.

The End

About The Author

Hi everyone I'm Tiffany Nixon!

I know you're curious to know how I started off as an author. It all started when I were twelve years old. I would write skits for myself and siblings to role play in front of our parents. As my writing skills improved, I decided I wanted to become a writer. At first, I doubted myself, thinking no one would read what a kid wrote. I was wrong!

The first poem I wrote was entered into a writing contest and I won first place. Ever since that day, I continued to write. Writing is my passion and I will forever remain faithful to it.

www.ingramcontent.com/pod-product-compliance
Lightning Source LLC
Chambersburg PA
CBHW070452170726
48291CB00005B/1716

* 9 7 8 1 9 4 7 9 2 8 4 0 4 *